FU MANCHU

Two Complete Adventures By
SAX ROHMER

Illustrated By
LEO O'MEALIA

Compiled And Edited By
TOM MASON

"The Zayat Kiss"
"The Severed Fingers"

Malibu Graphics, Inc.

Other books by Tom Mason

SPICY DETECTIVE STORIES
A classic collection of seven two-fisted pulp detective stories from the '30s

SPICY MYSTERY STORIES
Eight tales of mystery and suspense from Spicy Mystery magazine of the '30s.

ABBOTT & COSTELLO--The Classic Comics
Those wacky stars of stage, screen and television--Bud Abbott and Lou Costello--return in this mammoth collection of their best comic book adventures. More than 20 stories!

THE THREE STOOGES--The Knuckleheads Return!
Moe, Larry, and Curly return in the first of a series of trade paperbacks collecting their classic comic book adventures from the '40s to the '60s. Nyuk! Nyuk! Nyuk!

DAVE OLBRICH/Publisher • CHRIS ULM/Editor-In-Chief • MICKIE VILLA/Associate Editor • DAN DANKO/Assistant Editor
TOM MASON/Creative Director • Cover Coloring: Bruce Timm • Back Cover Coloring: Marcus David

---

SAX ROHMER
Two Complete Fu Manchu Adventures
Published by Malibu Graphics, Inc.
1355 Lawrence Drive #212
Newbury Park, CA 91320
805/499-3015

"Sax Rohmer and Fu Manchu" introduction copyright © 1989 John Wooley
All other contents copyright © 1989 Malibu Graphics, Inc. All rights reserved.
With the exception of artwork used for review pruposes, none of the contents
of this publication may be reproduced without the consent of Malibu Graphics, Inc.

Scott Rosenberg/President. Chris Ulm/Vice-President. Tom Mason/Secretary.
Dave Olbrich/Treasurer. Christine Hsu/Comptroller.

Printed in the U.S.A.
First Printing

ISBN #0-944735-24-X (Softcover) $9.95/$12.50 in Canada

SAX ROHMER AND FU MANCHU

Introduction by John Wooley

Somewhere around 80 years ago, Arthur Henry Sarsfield Ward went looking for a real-life Oriental mastermind in the dangerous and mysterious streets of London's Limehouse district. Ward didn't find the evil overlord he sought, but his experiences in those teeming streets led to the creation of the most famous "yellow menace" character in all of fiction, the insidious Dr. Fu Manchu.

Ward, born in Bimingham, England, in 1883, was, of course, better known by the pen name Sax Rohmer which he adopted in 1910— one year before publication of the first short story featuring Fu and three years before the first Fu Manchu novel hit the stands. That was *The Mystery of Dr. Fu Manchu*, and it introduced to the novel-reading public not only the cunning criminal mastermind but also his Scotland Yard nemesis, Sir Dennis Nayland Smith, and Smith's chum— and narrator of the stories— Dr. Petrie. Petrie's narration of the Fu Manchu tales calls to mind Dr. Watson's narration of Arthur Conan Doyle's Sherlock Holmes stories and it's probably no coincidence. The first Holmes book, *A Study in Scarlet*, was published in 1887 and by the turn of the century Holmes was just about the hottest thing in print.

Given Rohmer's lifelong interest in the occult— he was a member of the Hermetic Order of the Golden Dawn (along with the likes of Aleister Crowley and Arthur Machen) and wrote a reference book on the occult, *The Romance of Sorcery*, in 1914— it's interesting that the number 13 played such a role in the Fu Manchu series. Not only did the first book about Fu come out in 1913, but there were 13 novels in the series before Rohmer's death in 1959. Rohmer also wrote extensively in other areas, seeing more than 50 of his novels and short-story collections published in his lifetime, and writing plays, songs, comedy sketches, and magazine and newspaper articles as well.

It was in the latter capacity that he, in the early 1910s, ventured to the Limehouse district. On assignment for a newspaper, he was searching for a man known only as "Mr. King," a shadowy figure believed to be calling the shots for the entire criminal network of Limehouse, his fingers sunk deeply into, among other things, a vast drug-smuggling ring.

Rohmer trod the mysterious streets for months, running down leads, talking to shopkeepers, tracking the elusive, omnipotent Mr. King through darkened alleys, past peering and suspicious eyes. It was the kind of job that could form phantoms in the mind of a young journalist— and, apparently, that's exactly what happened. Because, although Rohmer never found Mr. King, the stories he heard and the sights he saw helped create the rich source material that formed the Fu Manchu stories.

One incident in particular coalesced all the Limehouse phantoms into one vision. In Vol. 3, No. 2 of *The Pulp Collector*, writer John Dinan quotes Rohmer from an unnamed source, as Rohmer talks about his Limehouse nights:

> I made many friends in the Chinese quarter, with its background of river noises, its frequent fogs, its sordid mystery. I found nothing to inspire romance. Then one night, and appropriately enough it was a foggy night, I saw a tall and very dignified Chinaman alight from a car. He was accompanied by an Arab girl, or she may have been an Egyptian, and as I saw the pair enter a mean-looking house, and as the fog drew a curtain over the scene, I conceived the character of Dr. Fu Manchu.

It was a character that would go on to be one of the most famous villains in all of literature, spawning movies as early as the 1920s and, for a couple of years, running in comic-strip form as well. That strip is resurrected here for the first time in more than half a century.

The artist who illustrated the Fu stories was Leo O'Mealia, a newspaper veteran who also figured into some of DC Comics' early efforts. The Fu Manchu strip, distributed by the Bell Syndicate, struggled along for awhile as a newspaper comic strip, died and was resurrected in the summer of 1938 as a reprint feature in DC's *Detective Comics*. Fu even got the cover on *Detective* #18.

O'Mealia, just prior to his *Fu Manchu* assignment, had drawn a *Sherlock Holmes* feature for syndication, which was not successful. After Fu, O'Mealia stayed for a time at DC doing new material, including covers for *Action Comics* and, for *New Fun Comics,* the series characters Bob Merritt and His Flying Pals and Barry O'Neill. The latter fought a running battle with a decidedly Fu-like villain called Fang Gow.

Fu Manchu disappeared from newspapers in 1932, and from *Detective Comics* in 1939, exiting the same issue that introduced a new costumed crimefighter known as the Batman. For the most part, he has stayed gone from the comics. The great Wally Wood drew and adaptation of *The Mask of Fu Manchu* in 1951; I.W. reprinted it 13 years later as *Dr. Fu Manchu.* And, in the 1970s, there was Fu's supporting role in the *Master of Kung Fu* series from Marvel. But things change, and not always for worse. The racial attitudes in America and England toward Far Eastern people are, these days, well-removed from the "yellow peril" mentality that flourished in the first few decades of this century, a mentality that helped give birth to Fu Manchu and his menacing yellow brethren in the pages of popular literature of the time.

Here, then, are adventures from another era, exotic, thrilling, and carrying with them the scent of jasmine, the whiff of mystery, and the whisper of dark, unfathomable menace.
—John Wooley

Thanks to James Vance for his help in preparing this introduction. John Wooley is the co-cretaor (with artist Terry Tidwell) of The Twilight Avenger, *a costumed super-hero not unfamiliar with the world of the '30s. He is currently adapting Edward D. Wood Jr's* Plan 9 From Outer Space *into graphic novel form with artists Stan Timmons and Bruce McCorkindale.*

"Imagine a man, tall, lean and cat-like, with long, strange, magnetic eyes, the brow of Shakespeare and the face of Satan... Invest him with the cruel cunning of an entire Eastern race, with all the resources of science, and vast wealth —imagine that awful being, and you have DR. FU MANCHU, the Yellow Peril incarnate in one man!"

Suddenly my old friend Nayland Smith put out the lamp. He had been explaining the mission that brought him surprisingly to my London quarters, when I supposed him to be in Burma. His tanned, square-jawed face was taut and grave. "A servant of the British Government, Petrie," he said, "I appear as a detective, bearing credentials from the highest sources, because I learned of the evil activity of FU MANCHU.

"No doubt you will think me mad," Smith remarked, and I could see him at the window peering intently into the street. "But before you are many hours older you will know I have good reason to be cautious . . . Ah, nothing suspicious!" He relighted the lamp. "You are the only man I can trust. I must have someone with me, Petrie, all the time. Can you spare a few days to the strangest business that ever was recorded in fact or fiction?" © 1931 By Sax Rohmer

"You're a doctor," Smith said, "Look at this!" He stripped off his coat. Rolling back his left shirt-sleeve he revealed a wicked-looking wound. "An arrow steeped in the venom of a hamadryad went in there."
A shudder I could not repress ran through me at his mention of that most deadly of all the reptiles of the East.

"Fu Manchu extracted the venom for that poisoned arrow from the glands of the snake. He caused me to be shot," continued Nayland Smith. "That fiend is now in London and I am on his tracks. I honestly believe that the interests of the entire white race depend upon the success of my mission." Then...

"I am wasting precious time," he rapped out. "We start now."
"What, tonight?"
"Tonight! I have scarcely slept in forty-eight hours, but there is one move that has to be made immediately. I must warn Sir Crichton Davey."
"Sir Crichton Davey—of the India—"

© 1931 By Sax Rohmer

We ran down the stairs. "Davey is a doomed man, Petrie," Smith told me as we hurried for a taxicab. "Unless he follows my instructions without question—before Heaven, nothing can save him! I do not know when the blow will fall, how, nor from whence, but I know that my first duty is to warn him."

"What's this?" muttered my friend hoarsely, as we approached Sir Crichton Davey's house. A little group of idlers hung about the steps. Without waiting for the cab to stop, Smith sprang out.

"What has happened?" he demanded breathlessly of a policeman.

4

Nayland Smith lurched back as though he had received a physical blow when the constable answered his question:
"Sir Crichton Davey has been killed, sir."
Beneath Smith's heavy tan his face had blanched, and his eyes were set in a stare of horror.
"I am too late!" he murmured.

With clenched fists Smith bounded up the steps. In the hall a Scotland Yard official was talking to a footman. Other members of the household were moving about aimlessly. The chill hand of King Fear had touched one and all, for, as they came and went they glanced over their shoulders, as if each shadow cloaked a menace....

© 1931 By Sax Rohmer

Smith strode up to the Scotland Yard man and showed him a card. The detective said something in a low voice, and saluted Smith in a respectful manner. After a few brief questions and answers we went upstairs and into the library, where Dr. Chalmers Cleeve was bending over a motionless form upon a couch.

The uncomfortable sense of hush, the group around the physician, the dead man—grim hub about whom all this activity turned—made a scene that etched itself indelibly on my mind. Then I observed another door, communicating with a small study. Through the opening I could see a man crawling on hands and knees examining the carpet...

As we entered the library, Dr. Cleeve straightened up from the couch where lay the body of Sir Crichton Davey. "This is a most mysterious case," he said. "Frankly, I do not care to venture any opinion now regarding the immediate cause of death. I fear that only a post-mortem can establish the facts—if we ever learn them!"

Sir Crichton's features were oddly puffy,, as were his clenched hands. He had been addicted to drugs, as Dr. Cleeve had told us, and as I pushed back the sleeve on his left arm, I saw the marks of the needle. Mechanically I looked at the right arm, which was unscarred. But on the back of the hand was a faint red mark, not unlike the impress of painted lips. .

Nayland Smith questioned Burboyne, Sir Crichton's secretary. The young man said he was working in the library that evening and his master was in the study, which was according to their usual custom. At ten twenty-five a district messenger brought a note for Sir Crichton, which Burboyne placed beside him on the study table. Except for that moment the door was closed.

"Suddenly," Burboyne recounted dramatically, "Sir Crichton burst open the door and threw himself with a scream into the library. I ran to him but he waved me back. His eyes were glaring horribly. . . .

"I had just reached his side when Sir Crichton fell writhing upon the floor," continued the nobleman's secretary. "He seemed past speech, but as I laid him upon the couch, he gasped something that sounded like 'The red hand!' From the direction of his last glance I think he referred to something in the study...

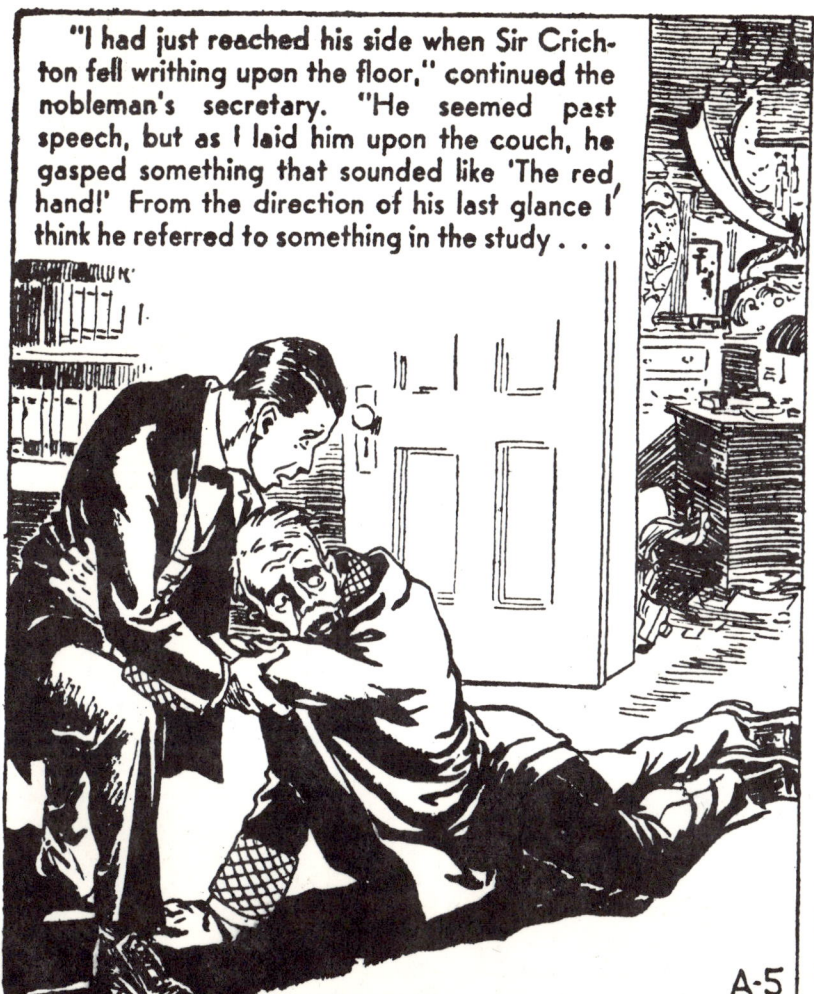

"Having called the servants I ran into the study. But there was absolutely nothing unusual to be seen. The windows were closed and fastened. There is no other door; anybody entering the study would have had to pass me. Even if somebody had been concealed, which would have been impossible in that small room, I should have seen him coming out."

Nayland Smith tugged at the lobe of his left ear, which was a habit of his when meditating.

"You had been at work here some weeks, I understand. Had anything unusual occurred?" he asked the secretary.

"Sir Crichton was writing an important book. He was very nervous, and something did happen, though I gave it little thought. . © 1931 By Sax Rohmer

"I searched the study three nights ago at the request of Sir Crichton, who thought something was hidden there."

"Some THING, or someone?" demanded Smith.

"The word he used was some THING!"

We entered Sir Crichton's study and Smith immediately pounced upon a large square envelope which lay beside the blotting pad upon the desk—no doubt the message which the secretary said had arrived at ten twenty-five. Sir Crichton had not bothered to open it, but Smith did so. It contained a blank sheet of paper!

"Smell!" Smith commanded me, thrusting the paper under my nose. It was scented with some pungent, rather sickish, perfume.

"What is it?" I asked.

"A somewhat rare essential oil. I've known it in the East. I think I begin to understand, Petrie."

As Nayland Smith tilted the lampshade and searched through the debris in the grate and on the hearth, I took up a copper vase and was examining it curiously....

"Put that back, old man," Smith said quietly.

Much surprised, I did as he directed.

"Don't touch anything in the room! It may be dangerous!"

Nayland Smith continued his careful search of the study in which Fu Manchu had caused the strange and dreadful death of Sir Crichton Davey. Smith was grim and wary as he looked in table drawers, back of the books, everywhere—like a man expecting at any moment to find something deadly. But the hunt proved vain.

In the hall we found a groom, who, at Smith's request, took us to the back of the house, where he had heard a cry at the time of Sir Crichton's death.

"Up there are the study windows, sir," the groom told Smith. "Over that wall is a lane from which the cry came."

"What was the cry like?" Smith asked, tensely.

"A sort of wail, sir," the frightened groom whispered. "I never heard anything like it before, and I never want to again."

"Was it like this?" inquired Smith, and uttered a low, wailing cry that made the flesh creep.

The groom shuddered at the eerie sound and so did I.

"It was the same cry, sir, but louder," the man said. "It came a moment after I saw Sir Crichton's shadow on the blind. . . . He was writing at his table . . . then he suddenly leaped up . . ."

Nayland Smith pointed to the house next door. "Those stairs lead from the kitchen to the servants' quarters, I presume," he said to the groom. "I am going to visit your neighbors." We went around to the front door in the square.

"I thought I had the start on Fu Manchu, but he is here before me," Smith said. "What is worse, his people have told him by now that I am here, too. Lounge up and down outside, Petrie. Keep your eyes open. Be on your guard!"

A white-faced butler admitted him to the house.

As I stood in the deserted square with time to think, the rapid events of the last hour seemed a nightmare. Smith's surprising arrival — his wound from a poisoned arrow—the dash to Sir Crichton's home—that cry of the dying man: "The red hand!"—the wail in the lane . . . all were like incidents of a delirium rather than reality . . .

Something touched me lightly on the shoulder . . . I turned, with my heart fluttering like a child's. The night's strange events had imposed a severe strain even upon my calloused doctor's nerves. . . . A girl wrapped in a hooded opera cloak stood at my elbow . . .

"Forgive me if I have startled you," the girl murmured, laying a slim, jeweled hand on my arm. "But—is it true—that Sir Crichton Davey has been murdered?"

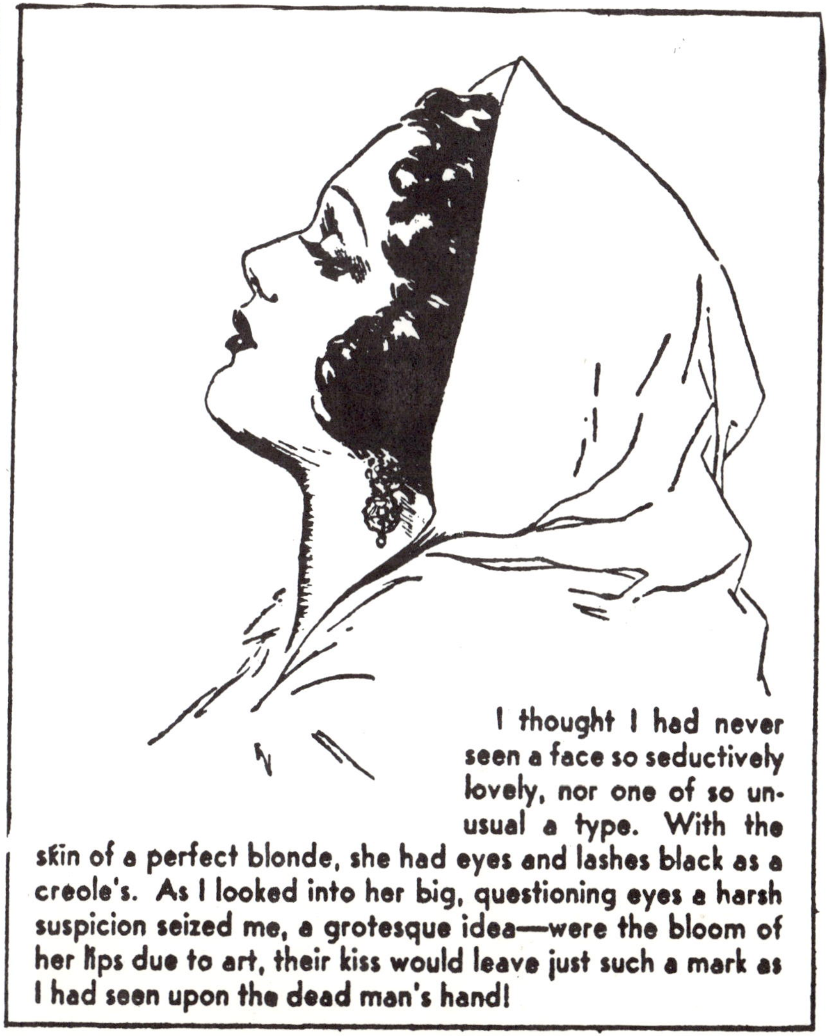

I thought I had never seen a face so seductively lovely, nor one of so unusual a type. With the skin of a perfect blonde, she had eyes and lashes black as a creole's. As I looked into her big, questioning eyes a harsh suspicion seized me, a grotesque idea—were the bloom of her lips due to art, their kiss would leave just such a mark as I had seen upon the dead man's hand!

But I dismissed the fantastic notion about the beautiful stranger as a fancy bred of the night's horrors. No doubt she was some friend or acquaintance of Sir Crichton Davey's. Acting on that idea, I sought to tell her what she asked as gently as I could.

"I cannot say he has been murdered," I told her, "but he is . . ."

"Dead?" she exclaimed huskily. I nodded. . . . The girl closed her eyes, and uttered a low moan, swaying dizzily . . .

"You are certain?" I asked her. "Let me walk with you until you feel quite sure of yourself."

She shook her head, flashed a glance at me with her beautiful eyes and looked away in a sort of sorrowful embarrassment. I was at a loss to account for her strange glance and demeanor—though I felt myself oddly thrilled..

The lovely girl smiled sadly from her slightly slanting, Oriental eyes, and pushed me gently away, when I threw my arm about her shoulders to support her, thinking she was about to faint.

"I am quite well, thank you," she said in a low, melodious voice.

Quickly she spoke again:
"I cannot let my name be mentioned in this dreadful matter, but—I think I have some information—for the police..."
She fumbled within the folds of her cloak.
"Will you give this to—whomever you think proper?"
The girl handed me a large sealed envelope....

As I stood mystified, the girl challenged my eyes with one of her dazzling glances... The next instant she had hurried away...

The girl had covered no more than ten or twelve yards when she turned abruptly and came running back. Without looking directly at me, but glancing alternately toward a far corner of the square and toward the house into which Nayland Smith had gone, she made an extraordinary request...

"If you would do me a very great personal service, for which I always would be grateful," she murmured haltingly, "when you have given my message to the proper person, leave him, and do not go near him any more tonight!"
She gazed straight into my eyes with passionate intentness...

Then she gathered up her cloak and fled, just as Nayland Smith ran down the steps. Before I could determine whether to follow her I heard the whir of a restarted motor at no great distance ... The girl's words had again aroused all my worst suspicions—

"She was a big card to play," Smith said, as he rejoined me.

"What! You know this girl? Who is she?"

"One of Fu Manchu's finest weapons!"

"But a woman is a two-edged sword, Petrie, and treacherous," Smith said to me. "To our great good-fortune she has formed a sudden attachment for yourself. That's the way with these Oriental women." He grinned. "And after all, Petrie, you are a handsome devil...."

"Scoff as much as you like," he added. "I've lived in the East—I know something about these strange, quick passions of the Oriental heart. She was employed by Fu Manchu to get this letter placed in my hands. He sent her on this errand."

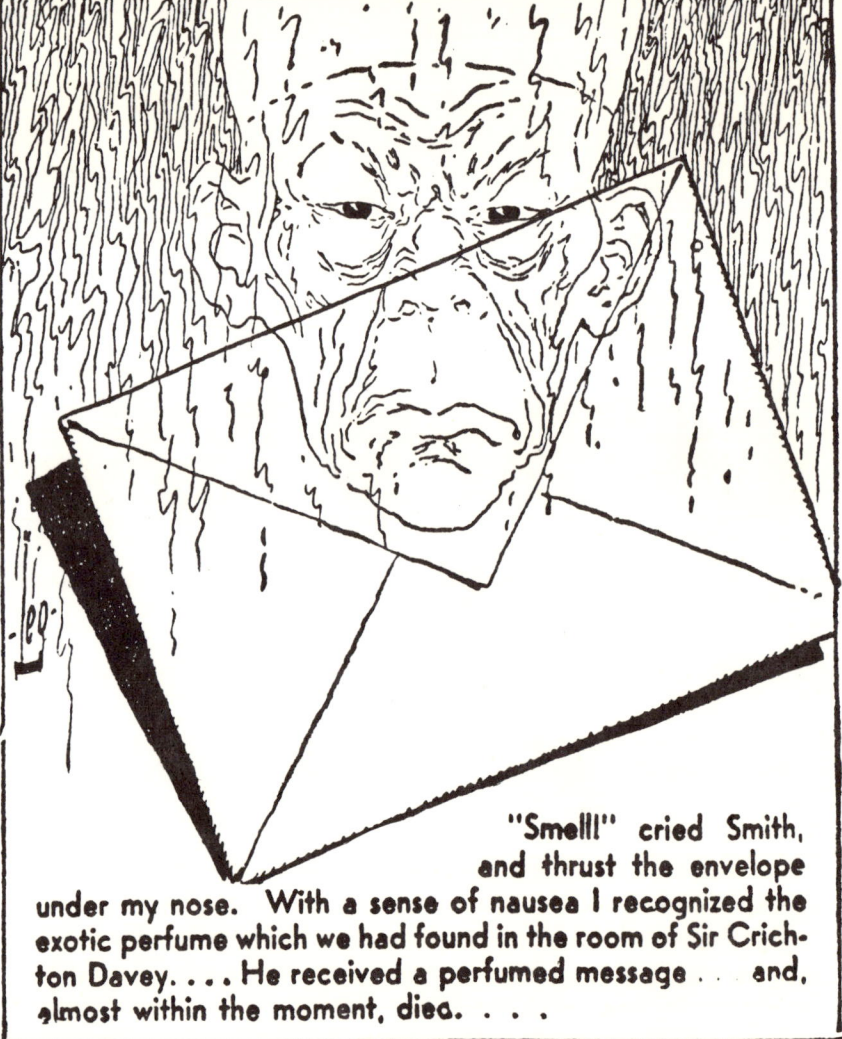

I contemplated the square of thick paper with horror.

"You know how an envelope exactly like this figured in the murder of Sir Crichton Davey The girl warned you, because she did not wish you to share my fate, Petrie. Can you doubt any longer that this beautiful girl has fallen in love with you?"

"Smell!" cried Smith, and thrust the envelope under my nose. With a sense of nausea I recognized the exotic perfume which we had found in the room of Sir Crichton Davey.... He received a perfumed message and, almost within the moment, died....

Holding gingerly the perfumed envelope—that message of death—which the mysterious girl had given to me, Nayland Smith led me toward a cab. "We're hardly safe from Fu Manchu here, Petrie," he said. "Get in quickly!"

Something whizzed past my ear, missed both Smith and me by a miracle, and whirled over the roof of the taxi with a hum like a hurled knife. "Attempt number one!" cried Smith, as we scrambled into the taxi. "If I escape alive from this business I shall know I bear a charmed life...."

"Tonight they will try to kill me," Smith said as we sank down on the cushions. He tapped the perfumed envelope. "Fu Manchu knows that I alone recognize him as the most evil and formidable personality in the world today, and understand how the yellow hordes of the East plot to destroy Western civilization . . . Look out of the back window, Petrie . . ."

"Someone has got into another cab," I whispered. "It is following ours!" © 1931 By Sax Rohmer

Smith filled his pipe and told me with a wry smile: "There is little to fear until we reach home. Then there is much." He went on to explain the terrifying movement controlled by Fu Manchu. "Why was Sir Crichton Davey murdered?" he asked. "He was one of those who would arouse the West to the menace of the awakening East...

"Sir Crichton died because, had the book upon which he was working ever seen the light, it would have disclosed him as the only living Englishman who understood the importance of the Tibetan frontiers...

"Why did M. Jules Furneaux fall dead in a Paris opera house? Heart failure? No! Fu Manchu! Furneaux's last speech had shown that he held the key to the secret of Tonking..."

What became of the Grand Duke Stanislaus? Elopement? Suicide? Nothing of the kind. He alone knew the truth about Mongolia. Fu Manchu caused him to vanish. I say to you solemnly, Petrie," Smith concluded, "that these are but a few. Is there a man who would reveal the Yellow plot, he shall die!"

"We have been followed here," I said to Smith when we reached my rooms." Why did you not try to throw them off the track?"

"Useless, Petrie," Smith laughed. "Wherever we went Fu Manchu would find us. And tonight I am to go to sleep unsuspecting, he believes, and die as Sir Crichton Davey died."

Smith threw the scented envelope upon the table, and shook his clenched fists toward the window.

"The villain!" he cried. "The fiendishly clever villain! I was too late to save Sir Crichton. But Fu Manchu has blundered..."

"What dreadful thing is hanging over your head?" I demanded. "What do these perfumed envelopes mean? How did Sir Crichton die?"
"He died of the ZAYAT KISS!"

"He does not guess I know the deadly peril of the perfumed message he sent by that mysterious girl. But I should have had the meaning of the 'information' from your charming friend, even if she had not warned you."
"Who is this girl?"
"Fu Manchu's daughter, wife—or most probably—his slave."

30

"Ask me what the Zayat Kiss may be," Nayland Smith went on, "and I reply 'I do not know.' The zayats are the Burmese caravanserais or rest-houses. In one of them on a certain route I set eyes on Fu Manchu for the first and last time. And in these rest-houses travelers sometimes die like Sir Crichton Davey, with nothing to show the cause except a little mark which has got the name of the Zayat Kiss . . .

"I have my theory, Petrie, and hope to prove it tonight—if I live. It will be one more broken weapon in Fu Manchu's devilish armory. I wanted to study the Zayat Kiss in operation, and I shall have the chance."

"But the scented envelopes?" I inquired.

"In the swampy forests of the Burmese district I have mentioned grows a green orchid with a peculiar scent. I recognized the heavy perfume at once. I take it that the thing which kills the traveler is attracted by this orchid. The perfume clings to whatever it touches..."

"Fu Manchu no doubt has a supply of the green orchids — probably to feed the creature."
"What creature?"

Smith did not immediately answer my question about Fu Manchu's sinister pet, but said: "I found this strange contrivance on Sir Crichton's roof near the chimney of his study fireplace." He drew from his pocket a tangled length of silk thread, mixed up with which were a brass ring, and a number of large split shot, nipped on the silk in the manner usual on a fishing line.

"This explains how the thing got into Sir Crichton's study," Smith explained. "The shot were to weight the line and prevent the creature from clinging to the side of the chimney. When it had dropped in the grate, the weighted line was withdrawn, and the thing was held only by one single thread, which sufficed to draw it back when it had done its fatal work...."

33

"They reckoned that the creature would make straight up the leg of the table, toward the prepared envelope..."

"What is your theory about the creature—what shape, what color?"

"It is something that moves rapidly. It works in the dark—the study was dark except for the light on the table..."

"From the table-leg to the hand of Sir Crichton—which, having touched the envelope, was scented with the perfume—was a certain move for the creature..."

"How horrible!"

"Sir Crichton saw the thing—leaped up—and received the ZAYAT KISS!"

34

A-18

"Let us make ostentatious preparations to retire, Petrie," Nayland Smith said coolly, "and I think we can rely on Fu Manchu's servants to attempt my removal—if not yours, also—by means of the Zayat Kiss."
"But it's a climb of thirty-five feet to our windows!"

"You remember the call in the lane when Sir Crichton died," replied Smith, leading the way into the bedroom. "It is a dacoit—an East Indian murderer—who operates the Zayat Kiss. The ivy, you know, runs all the way up to the window. To a dacoit an ivy-covered wall is a grand staircase...." © 1931 By Sax Rohmer

Smith put the perfumed envelope on a little table in the middle of the room. We stuffed coats and rugs under the covers of the bed to give the appearance of a sleeper...

Smith squatted on cushions in a shadowy corner, with a revolver and an electric pocket-lamp. He also laid a golf club beside him. As I switched out the light, the utter silence was broken by a distant clock striking two...

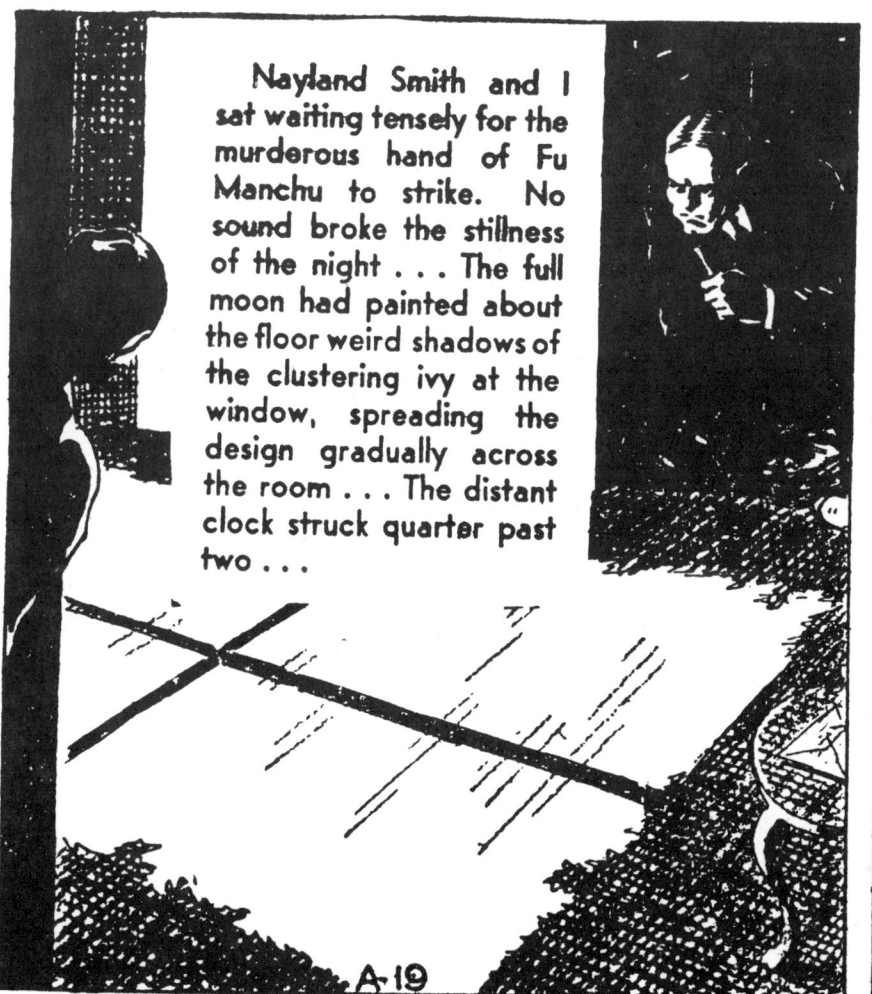

Nayland Smith and I sat waiting tensely for the murderous hand of Fu Manchu to strike. No sound broke the stillness of the night... The full moon had painted about the floor weird shadows of the clustering ivy at the window, spreading the design gradually across the room... The distant clock struck quarter past two...

A slight breeze stirred the ivy, and the shadows spread further. The moonlight now touched the little table where lay the sinister perfumed envelope which was to lure to its deadly task the thing that dealt the Zayat Kiss... The faraway half-hour sounded....

I pictured Fu Manchu, awaiting in some mysterious hiding place the outcome of this monstrous attempt to end Nayland Smith's war against his villainies... A shudder swept me at the thought of the Yellow genius of evil...

The clock struck three... Something rose, inch by inch, above the sill of the window...

Now the figure at the window cast a shadow on the floor in the form of a man. The moment for which Nayland Smith and I waited had come . . . I was icy cold, expectant, prepared for whatever horror might be upon us . . .

A sibilant breath from Smith told me that he, from his post, could see the cause of the shadow, which became stationary. It was the dacoit who operated the Zayat Kiss. He was studying the interior of the room . . .

There was absolutely no sound at the window, but the lithe form of a man clung there in the moonlight. A yellow face was pressed against the panes...

Thin hands raised the sash. One hand disappeared, and reappeared in a moment grasping a small, square box...
There was a very faint *click*...

There was something so murderously ominous in that faint click from the black box that Nayland Smith and I leaped to our feet ... The dacoit swung himself below the window with the agility of an ape as, with a dull, muffled thud, *something* dropped upon carpet! The Zayat Kiss ... Fear prickled my spine ... In the very room with us was that nameless creature which Fu Manchu had dispatched on its errand of death....

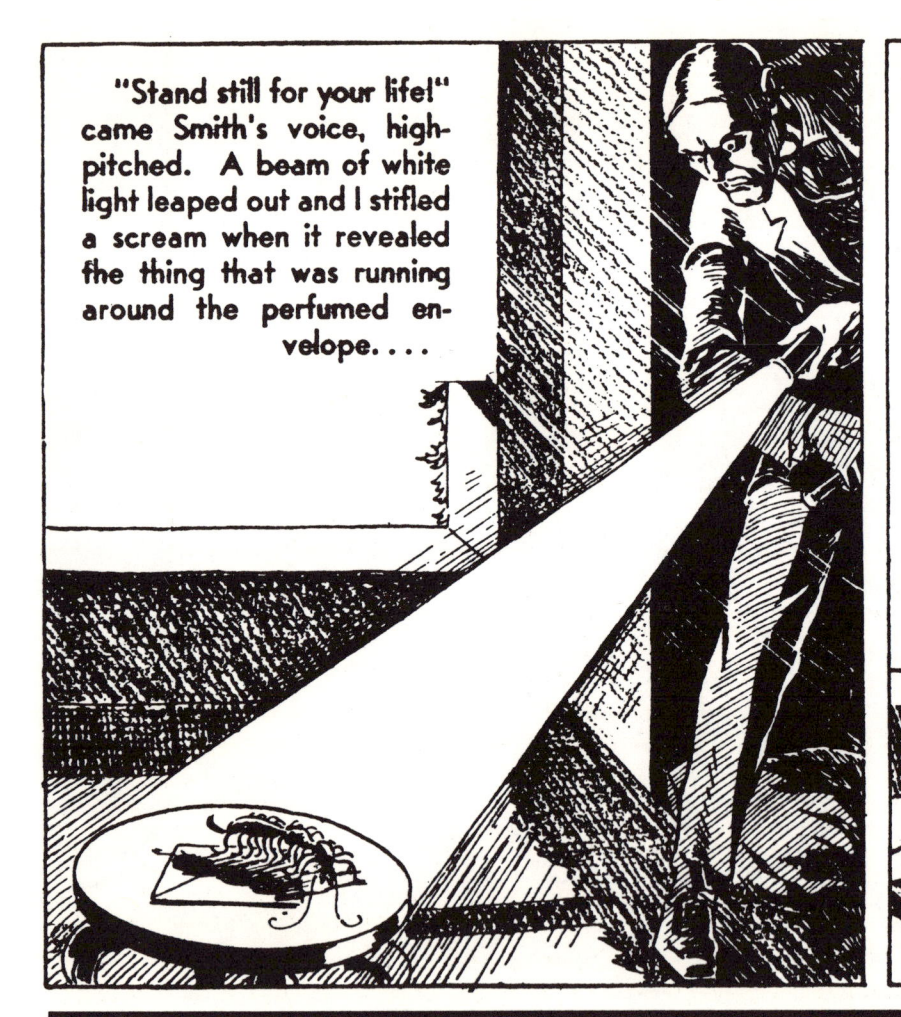

"Stand still for your life!" came Smith's voice, high-pitched. A beam of white light leaped out and I stifled a scream when it revealed the thing that was running around the perfumed envelope....

As Smith advanced with the golf-club raised I saw the terrible creature was an insect, full six inches long, of a vivid, venomous, red color! It had something the appearance of a great ant, with its long, quivering antennae and its febrile, horrible vitality. But it was a giant centipede, with numberless, rapidly moving legs....

All the ghastliness of Fu Manchu's diabolical plot to destroy us by means of the Zayat Kiss I realized in one breathless instant. In the next, Nayland Smith, with one straight, true blow of the golf club had dashed out the thing's poisonous life!

A-22

"The window, Petrie!" cried Smith, and I ran to it... As I did so I felt brushing my hand the silken thread which had been the giant centipede's tether....

Drawing my pistol, I leaned far out over the window ledge, Smith at my elbow.... But we were too late....

Looking down the wall we could see the dacoit dropping with incredible agility from branch to branch of the ivy. Without offering a mark for a shot, Fu Manchu's servant of death melted into the shadows beneath the garden's trees....

Nayland Smith dropped limply into a chair as I turned on the light. Even his grim courage had been sorely tried in thwarting Fu Manchu's hideous plot against our lives.

I had gone back to the window and was gazing out again, hoping for a glimpse of our late visitor. Smith joined me there. "Never mind the dacoit, Petrie," he said. "Nemesis will know where to find him."

We stood looking aghast at what was left of the deadly insect from which Smith's golf club had saved us. "We know now what causes the mark of the Zayat Kiss," he said. "Therefore science is richer for our first brush with the enemy, and the enemy is poorer—unless Fu Manchu has more centipedes...."

"And another mystery is solved, Petrie," Smith added eagerly. "Now I understand something that has puzzled me ever since the night Sir Crichton Davey was murdered. As he staggered dying from his study, you remember, he uttered a stifled cry...."

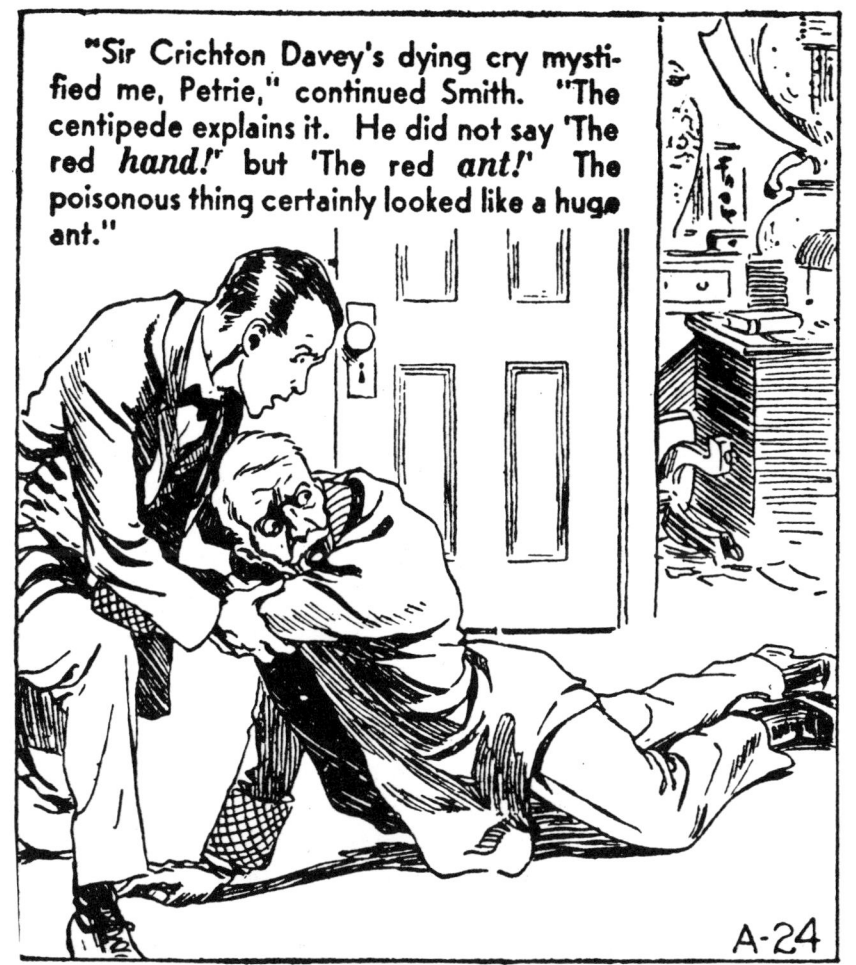

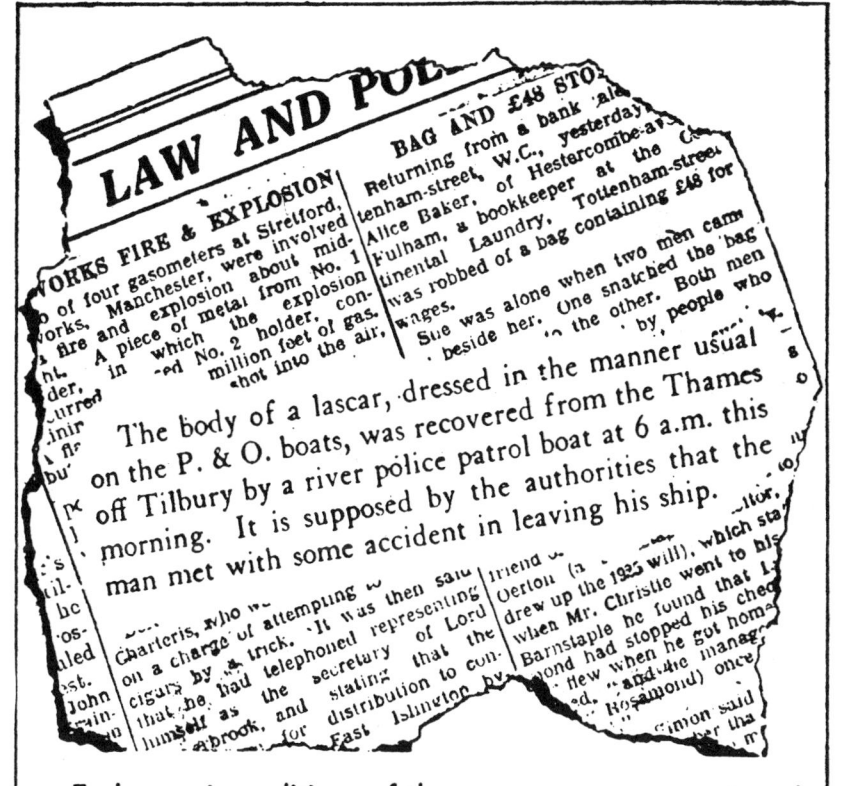

"Sir Crichton Davey's dying cry mystified me, Petrie," continued Smith. "The centipede explains it. He did not say 'The red *hand!*' but 'The red *ant!*' The poisonous thing certainly looked like a huge ant."

A-24

Early evening editions of the newspapers were out next day before Smith and I had slept our fill after the night's strange and exciting events. Smith passed me a paper indicating a paragraph among the minor police items.

"For '*lascar*' read '*dacoit*'" Smith said. "Our caller who came by way of the ivy failed to accomplish his purpose, luckily for us. Also, he lost the centipede and left a clue behind. Dr. Fu Manchu does not overlook such lapses...."

My thoughts recoiled from consideration of the fate that would be ours if ever we fell into the clutches of this evil being!

It was an indication of our jangled nervous state that we both started from our chairs as the telephone rang.

"It's Inspector Weymouth of New Scotland Yard," I told Smith. "He wants you...."

NAYLAND SMITH, British Government official, is in London from the East fighting Dr. Fu Manchu, sinister leader of a vast Yellow conspiracy to overthrow Western civilization. Fu Manchu, having murdered Sir Crichton Davey with the Zayat Kiss, seeks to end the lives of Smith and Dr. Petrie, his associate, by the same means. But they kill Fu Manchu's poisonous giant centipede. Now...

Nayland Smith and I were quickly ready to respond to Inspector Weymouth's urgent summons to the Wapping River Police Station. Peaceful interludes were rare and brief in our pursuit of Fu Manchu.

"It is certainly something important, Petrie," said Smith as we waited for a taxi to pull up, "and it is probably ghastly if Fu Manchu is at the bottom of it." At the police station we were taken immediately to Inspector Weymouth. Greeting us briefly, he nodded toward a long table, where lay a still form.

"Poor Cadby!" Weymouth said, his usually gruff voice softened. "He was one of the most promising detectives at Scotland Yard."
"Fu Manchu!" half-whispered Smith.
"Look!" I cried in horror.
Three fingers of the left hand were missing.

"You noticed the fingers?" asked the Inspector. "It was almost the same with Detective Mason. He went off a week ago on some business of his own. Next night the ten-o'clock boat got the grapnel on him off Hanover Hole. His first two fingers on the right hand were completely gone."

I looked out at the whispering Thames, which held so many secrets, and now was burdened with another. Behind me I heard the Inspector say:
"And that lascar we found this morning..."
"You mean Fu Manchu's dacoit," interjected Smith, "He tried to kill Petrie and me."
"He was minus half his fingers, too...."

Smith strode up and down the neat little room. I turned to the array of objects found in Detective Cadby's clothing. None of them was noteworthy except that which had been found thrust into the loose neck of the shirt—and had led the police to send for Nayland Smith because the clue pointed to Fu Manchu...

"Smith," I cried, "what do you make of this?"

It was a Chinese pigtail. That was remarkable enough; but the plaited queue was a false one, attached to a most ingenious bald wig!

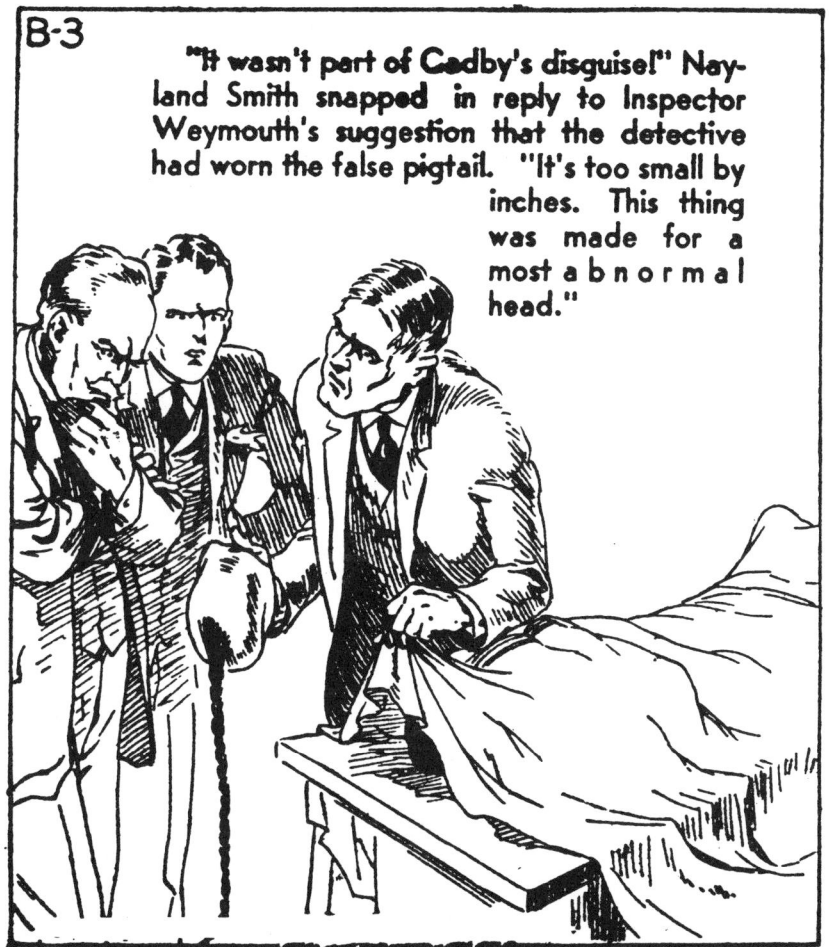

B-3 "It wasn't part of Cadby's disguise!" Nayland Smith snapped in reply to Inspector Weymouth's suggestion that the detective had worn the false pigtail. "It's too small by inches. This thing was made for a most abnormal head."

"Where did you find Cadby?" Smith asked the Inspector.
"Limehouse Reach—under Commercial Dock, exactly an hour ago," he replied, and added that Cadby had been on some mission in the Ratcliff Highway section on the previous evening. "He died from drowning, yet he was a good swimmer. So was the other victim, Mason."

"Then we know that Cadby was hot on the trail of the Fu Manchu group in the Ratcliff Highway neighborhood last night," Smith summed up. "Mason probably blundered on the same scent and met a similar fate. They almost succeeded where we failed, Petrie..."

"Fu Manchu had the dacoit killed, and these men died in the same way," Smith concluded. "Let us hope that some day we shall know how they died."

I was aghast and puzzled at this series of hideous crimes.

"What is the meaning of the mutilated hands?" I demanded of Smith.

Inspector Weymouth handed Nayland Smith Cadby's keys and a card with the detective's address, after telling us where to find Cadby's case-book. "We haven't a second to waste, Petrie," Smith said. "Fu Manchu wants those records, too!"

But we had ridden only a few hundred yards along Wapping High Street when Smith called to the driver: "Stop! Stop!" He seized the door-handle as the cab slowed down. "We must have it, Petrie," he cried. "I have left it behind. That pigtail!"

At the cab door Smith handed me Weymouth's card. "Don't wait for me," he directed hurriedly. "Remember Weymouth said the book was in the cupboard. It's all we want. Meet me at Scotland Yard."

Cadby's case-book, with its damning evidence, was it already in Fu Manchu's hands? "Do you think Fu Manchu is going to leave dynamite like that lying around?" Smith had argued. "It's a thousand to one he has the book already, but there is just a bare chance . . ."

With the remorseless memories of Fu Manchu's murders harrowing my mind, I reached the house of his latest victim. The shadow of that giant evil seemed to lie upon it like a palpable cloud. I ran up the steps and rang the bell...

Cadby's landlady greeted me with a queer mixture of fear and embarrassment. "I am Dr. Petrie," I said, "and I have bad news about your lodger, Mr. Cadby."

"Oh the poor, brave lad!" she murmured.

"There was a terrible waiting at the back of the house last night," the woman told me excitedly as we entered the hall. "And I heard it again tonight, a second before you rang...."

Fu Manchu! A dacoit had wailed in the lane when Sir Crichton Davey died....

I told the old lady what I considered necessary about Cadby's death, and presently, to my astonishment, her grief was lost in embarrassment. Then the truth came out!

She pointed shakily up the stairs, and stammered:

"There's a—young lady—in his rooms, sir!"

"The girl came and waited for Mr. Cadby last night," the landlady said as I started up the stairs. "This morning she came again, and the third time an hour ago. Not the kind of girl I'd want a son of mine to take up with . . . But those dark eyes. . ."

Could I forget the dark eyes of the strange girl who had given me a deadly message that night of the Zayat Kiss—and told me to beware? Was that lure of men even now in the house, completing her evil work? The waiting of the dacoit—it was surely a warning of a stranger's approach . . .

There was a soft rustling at the head of the stairs. The girl was stealing down! But at a glimpse of me she fled. I followed, and bounded into the room above almost at her heels. She cowered against the desk, a slim figure in a clinging silk gown . . .

Fear enhanced her startling beauty and lit to even more dazzling brilliance the wonderful eyes of this modern Delilah.

"So I came in time," I said grimly, and turned the key in the lock.

The girl stood facing me in Detective Cadby's room.

"Give me whatever you have removed from here," I commanded, "and then prepare to accompany me."

B-7

She was Fu Manchu's servant, yet her charm enveloped me like a magic cloud. I had laughed when Nayland Smith spoke of this girl's infatuation for me, but now, in her pleading eyes, I read confirmation of his words...

I steeled myself. Cadby's book—the evidence against Fu Manchu— "What have you taken from here?" I demanded.

"I have taken nothing, Dr. Petrie," she cried.

"You have no claim to mercy," I told her.

"Oh, let me go! Please let me go!" she panted. And impulsively the girl threw herself forward, pressing clasped hands against my shoulder, and looking up into my face with warm, pleading eyes..

Her beauty was wholly intoxicating, but I thrust her away, and she sank pitifully to the floor.

"I will tell you all I can, all I dare, Dr. Petrie," she cried eagerly, fearfully. "If you only understood — y o u would not be so cruel..."

"I am not free. What I do, I must, for I am Fu Manchu's slave. Ah, you are not a man if you can give me to the police—if you can forget I tried to save you once..."

I turned my back toward her. How could I give her up—perhaps to stand trial for murder? Certainly she had tried to save me from the awful danger of the Zayat Kiss. . .

Suddenly she raised herself to her knees, weeping. "It is not your work to hound a woman to death!" she cried. "Ah, I have no friend in all the world. Have mercy on me! Be my friend and save me—from Fu Manchu!"

64

The girl regarded me with her soul in her eyes, in an abandonment of pleading despair. Must I betray her? Her seductive beauty argued against my sense of right . . .

Then I remembered the fate of the man in whose room we stood.

"You lured Cadby to his death!" I accused her.

"No! No!" she screamed, wildly. "No! I swear by the holy name I did not . . .

"I watched him, spied upon him—yes! But listen, Dr. Petrie! It was because he would not be warned that he met his death. I could not save him. I am not so bad as that . . .

"I took his note-book," she went on breathlessly. "It was too big to steal away. I tore out the pages and burned them in the grate . . ."

"There, will you let me go now?" the slave-girl finished.
"Yes, if you will tell me how to seize Fu Manchu."
A new terror came into her face.
"I dare not! I dare not!" she gasped.

Suddenly she came close and whispered in my ear: "Could you hide me from Fu Manchu, from the police, from everybody, if I came to you and told you all I know?"
I felt the hot blood leap to my cheek at all that the words implied . . .

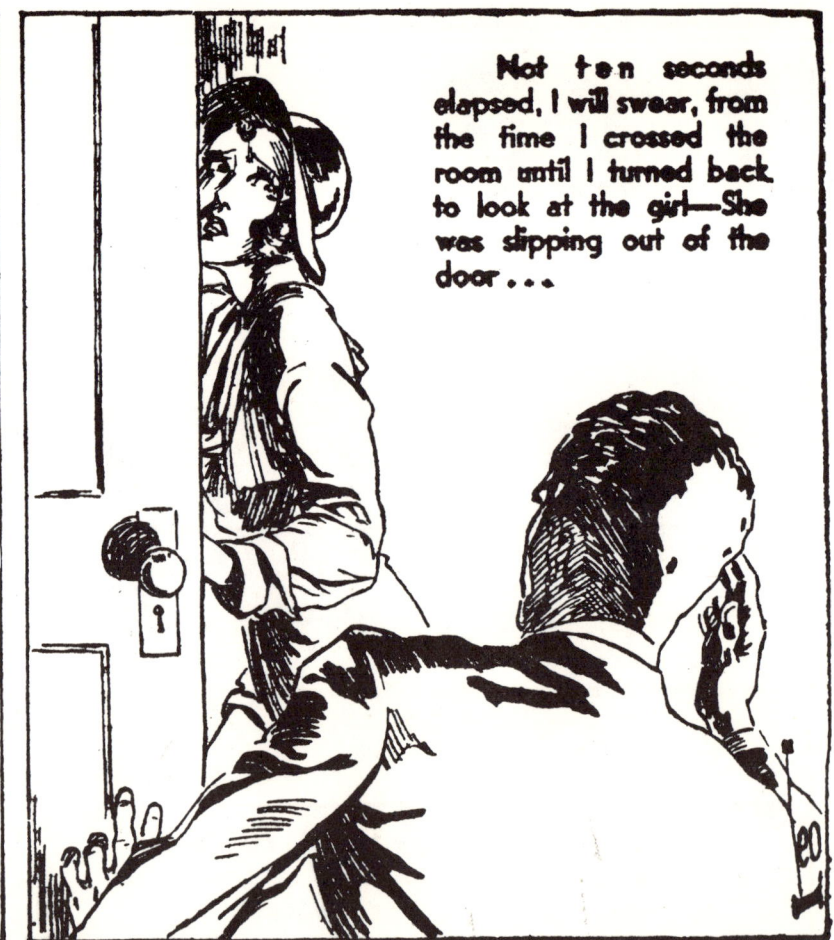

I turned away from her toward the fireplace. I had not counted on this warring with a woman. What could I do? What should I do? By the charm of her personality and the art of her pleading this girl had made it all but impossible for me to give her up to justice...

Not ten seconds elapsed, I will swear, from the time I crossed the room until I turned back to look at the girl—She was slipping out of the door...

As I leaped to the door through which the strange girl had vanished in the twinkling of an eye, I heard the key turned gently from the outside.

"I am sorry, Dr. Petrie," came her soft whisper from against the panels, "but I am afraid to trust you—yet. Be comforted, for there is one near who would have killed you had I only wished it, and said just one little word. . . . Remember, I will come to you whenever you will take me and hide me."

Tricked! So that was how I had served Nayland Smith on this important mission. Bewitched by a woman! Well — another time. Meanwhile, the fireplace....

Stooping over the fireplace I gave a cry of triumph. So hurriedly had the girl done her work that some charred fragments were still left of Detective Cadby's evidence against Fu Manchu.... Evidently she had burned the torn-out pages all together. They lay flat, and the middle portion did not burn. What would this find reveal?

Nayland Smith and I were in Inspector Weymouth's room at Scotland Yard whither I had hurried from Detective Cadby's room.

"Shen-Yan's is a dope shop off Ratcliff Road," said the Inspector. "'Singapore Charlie's,' they call it. It's a center for Chinese societies. But..."

All three of us bent again over a large sheet of foolscap upon which were arranged some of the charred fragments I had salvaged from Detective Cadby's grate. They comprised a baffling puzzle over which we had been mulling for minutes.

"Well, let's see what we make of this," said Smith.

Weymouth picked up one of the fragments between a stubby thumb and finger.
"The pigtail again!" he exclaimed.

"Detective Cadby, who was outside in disguise, saw a lascar go upstairs at Shen-Yan's," Nayland Smith told Inspector Weymouth and me after pondering the puzzle of the charred scraps from Cadby's record-book.

"Cadby heard a booming sound," Smith continued. "Undoubtedly that had something to do with the fact that the 'lascar' didn't come down again. For I am sure the 'lascar' was the dacoit who tried to kill Petrie and me with the Zayat Kiss—and whose body was dragged from the river . . .

"This was found on Detective Cadby's body, so his reference to a pigtail is highly interesting—also mysterious..." Nayland Smith wrinkled his brow in deep thought... Suddenly he squared his shoulders as one reaching a decision...

"You must lend me a disguise," Smith announced grimly to the astonished Inspector Weymouth. "I visit Shen Yan's opium den tonight!"

"Shen Yan's! That's dangerous business!" Inspector Weymouth protested at Nayland Smith's announcement that he would go to the opium den where we suspected Fu Manchu lurked. "How about an official visit by the police?"

"Fu Manchu is the incarnate essence of Chinese craftiness. Such a visit would be useless!" Smith snapped. "No! We must match guile with guile."

"Well, if you're determined sir," the Inspector agreed. "Foster will fix you up."

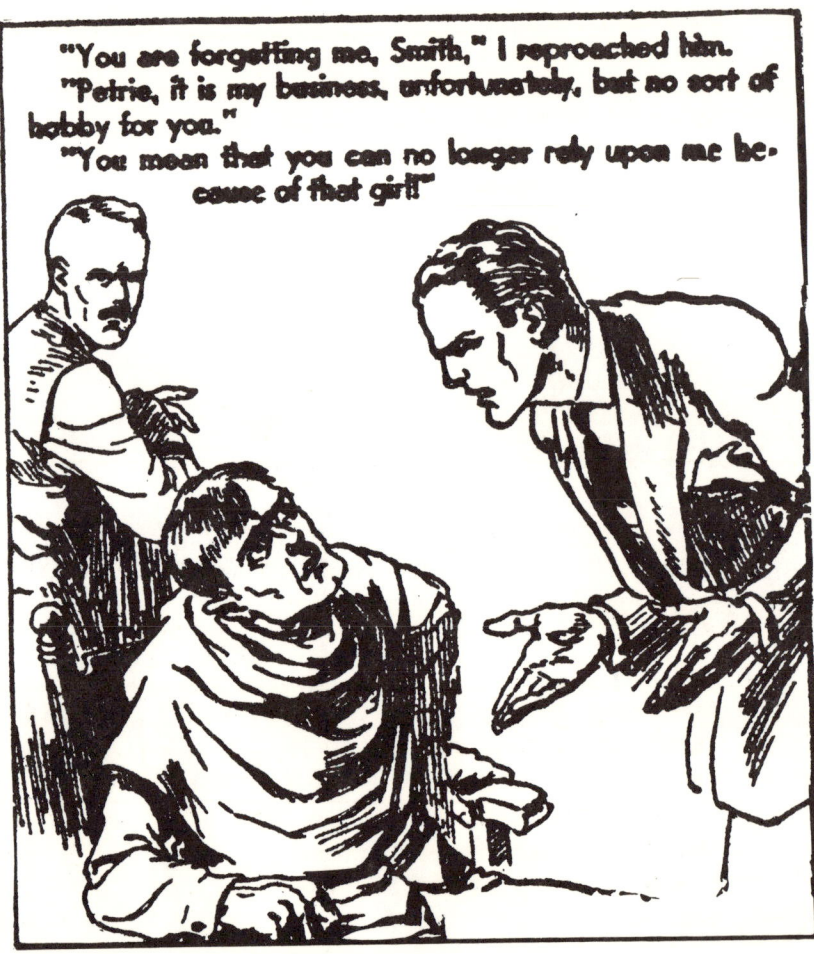

Foster came with a seaman's rig, and I watched the transformation of Smith into a sinister waterfront character.... Recollection of how I had let the slave girl trick me made my heart heavy...

"You are forgetting me, Smith," I reproached him.
"Petrie, it is my business, unfortunately, but no sort of hobby for you."
"You mean that you can no longer rely upon me because of that girl!"

76

Nayland Smith met my frigid stare with a look of concern.

"My dear old Petrie," he answered. "That was really unkind... I was thinking of the danger to you...."

"I shall be going, too, Inspector," I called to Weymouth, for I was immediately ashamed of my outburst. "I can pretend to smoke opium as well as you," I told Smith.

In a little while two seafaring ruffians were ready to set forth.

"Observe my fine mustache, Petrie," Smith said with a grin as we went out to the cab. I could have laughed aloud, there was something so ridiculous in this theatrical business. Then I remembered Fu Manchu!

Fu Manchu awaited us at our journey's end! With all the powers of Nayland Smith pitted against him, Fu Manchu pursued his devilish schemes triumphantly, and hid within this very area we approached. Fu Manchu, whose name stood for horrors indefinable! Was I destined to meet the terrible Chinese doctor—tonight?

78

Four shabby fellows saluted when we entered the Wapping River Police Station. We were to go to Shen Yan's in the police launch, which would await an alarm from us. "But don't wait too long," Weymouth warned Smith, when plans were completed, "or you may appear next in the river with half your fingers missing."

Shortly we were ready to go. According to instructions, one of the shabby detectives already lay in a feigned drunken sleep near Shen Yan's dope shop, while his comrade argued with him to get up. "Don't move till you hear the whistle inside," the Inspector had told them.

The other two sleuths, acting on their orders, had broken from the back into an empty shop opposite Shen Yan's. "Be inside Shen Yan's like lightning when you hear the signal," were Weymouth's parting words to them.

"The launch is ready, sir," announced Inspector Ryman from the doorway, and we trooped out to the little craft. The chill of the water penetrated my thin garments.... I thought of Fu Manchu... the Severed Fingers ... as we headed into the shadows...

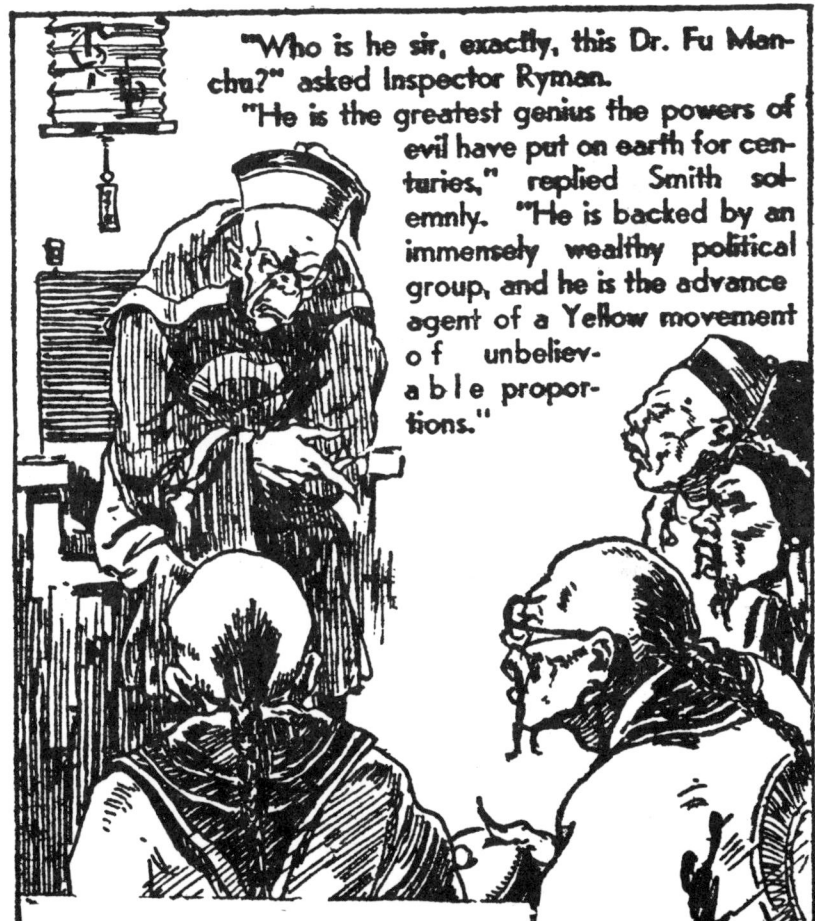

Aboard the police launch on the way to Shen Yan's, Nayland Smith told Inspector Ryman, in command: "I'm not sure Fu Manchu is there tonight, but the opium den appears to be one of his haunts, and time means precious lives where this Chinese devil is concerned."

"Who is he sir, exactly, this Dr. Fu Manchu?" asked Inspector Ryman.

"He is the greatest genius the powers of evil have put on earth for centuries," replied Smith solemnly. "He is backed by an immensely wealthy political group, and he is the advance agent of a Yellow movement of unbelievable proportions."

We went on deck as the launch drew closer in toward the murky shore, and Inspector Ryman ordered: "On your left, past the wooden pier! Not where the lamp is; beyond that, next to the dark square building, Shen Yan's."

Smith was first ashore. "Lie close in, with your ears open," he told Inspector Ryman.
From his voice I knew this night mystery of the Thames, the threat of Fu Manchu's nearness, had unstrung even Smith's iron nerves....

Nayland Smith lurched in halting fashion toward the door of the little shop which we hoped and believed was the entrance to the hiding-place of Fu Manchu. I shuffled along behind him...

SHEN YAN
BARBER

Smith kicked the door open and clattered down three wooden steps. Suddenly he pulled himself up with a jerk, seizing my arm for support....

We stood in a bare and very dirty room, which could only claim kinship with a civilized barber shop by virtue of the grimy towel thrown across the back of the solitary chair. At the back was a curtain brocaded with filth....

As Smith and I stood regarding this ominous place with all our senses alert, the grimy curtain parted and the face of a Chinaman peered out at us....

The Chinaman who approached Nayland Smith and me from behind the curtained doorway in Shen Yan's, chattered like a monkey: "No shavee! Too late! Shuttee shop!" We guessed this was Shen Yan.

Smith shook his fist under Shen Yan's chin, and roared: "Get inside an' gimme an' my mate a couple o' pipes. Smokee pipe, you yellow scum! Savvy?"

"Allee lightee," the Chinaman said. "Full up, no room. You come see." He dived behind the curtain, Smith and I following. He ran up a dark stair. The next moment I found myself in a room which reeked with opium fumes...

A tin oil lamp on the floor lit the horrible place, about the walls of which were ten or twelve bunks. One or two occupants sucked at their opium pipes, but the rest lay motionless—drugged...

Nayland Smith dropped cross-legged on the floor of the opium den. I squatted beside him. "Two pipe quick," he said to our guide, after thrusting a coin into his yellow paw—"Or plenty heap trouble."

Shen Yan shuffled to the smoky lamp. Holding a long needle in the flame he dipped it into an old cocoa tin. A bead of opium adhered to the end. Roasting the drug over the lamp, he dropped it into the bowl of a pipe which he held ready...

"Pass it over!" called Smith huskily, with the assumed eagerness of a slave to the drug. He put the pipe to his lips, while Shen Yan prepared another for me.
"Whatever you do, don't inhale any, Petrie!" he warned.

We pretended to smoke, and taking my cue from Smith I allowed my head gradually to sink lower and lower, until, within a few minutes, I sprawled sideways on the floor, Smith close by me.

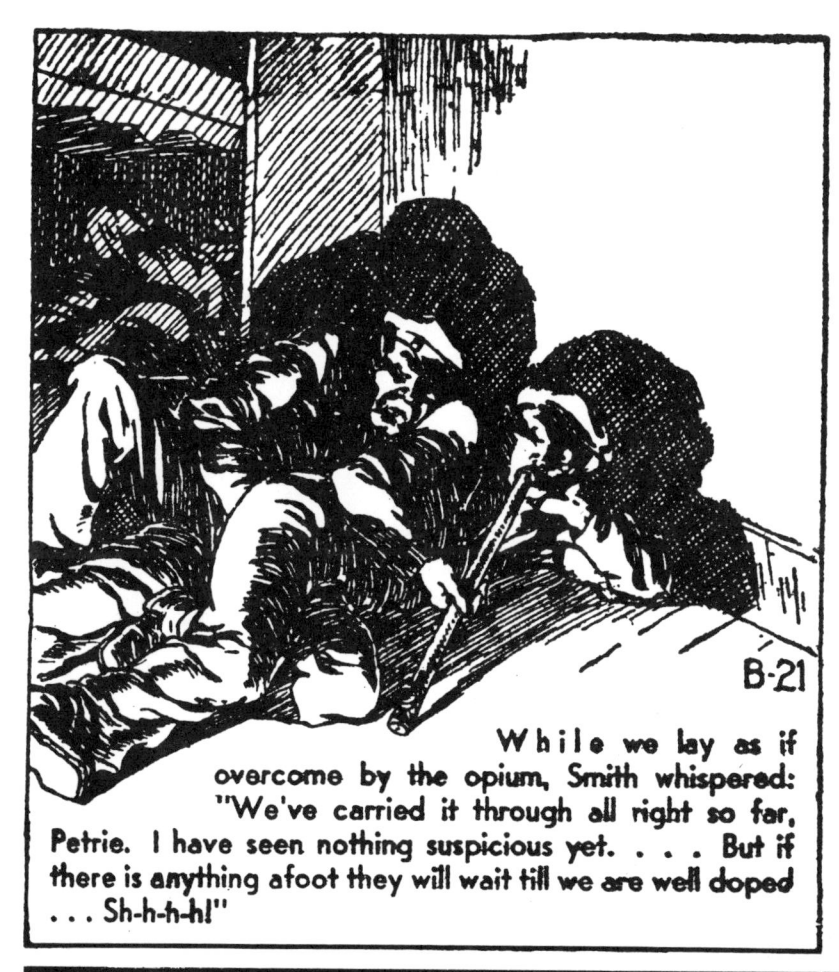

While we lay as if overcome by the opium, Smith whispered: "We've carried it through all right so far, Petrie. I have seen nothing suspicious yet. . . . But if there is anything afoot they will wait till we are well doped . . . Sh-h-h-h!"

A form parted the curtain of a stairway near us. From the sprawling shapes all about rose strange sighings and murmurings . . . The newcomer was slight and hunched, with a misshapen pigtailed head. There was something unnatural, inhuman, about the mask-like face. . . .

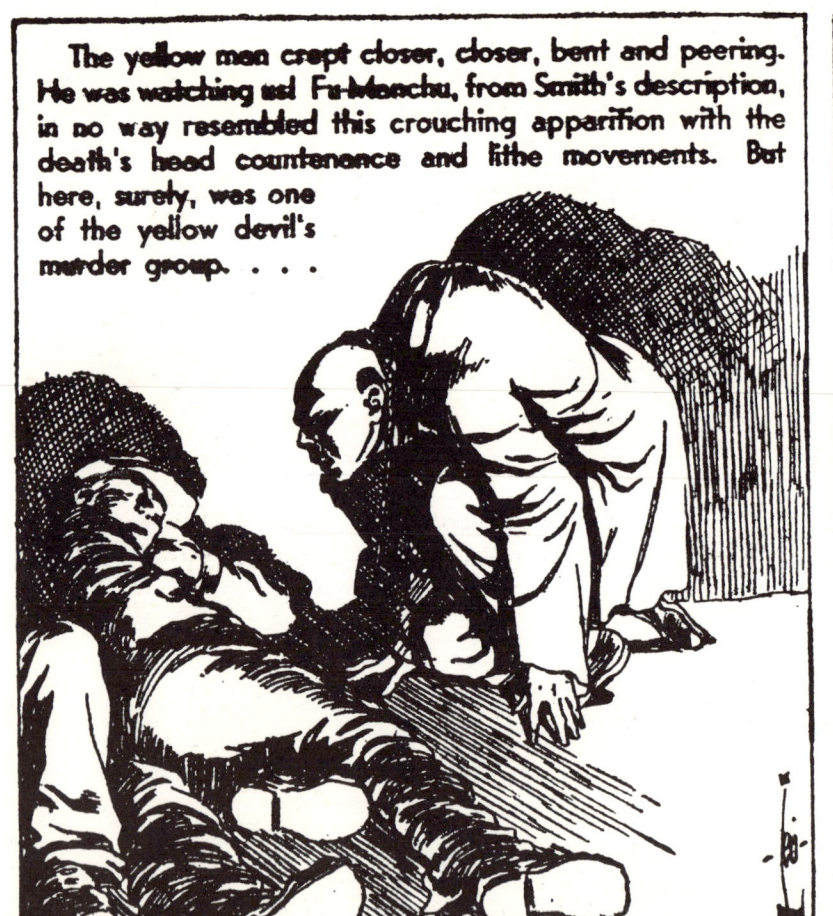

The yellow man crept closer, closer, bent and peering. He was watching us! Fu-Manchu, from Smith's description, in no way resembled this crouching apparition with the death's head countenance and lithe movements. But here, surely, was one of the yellow devil's murder group....

Through barely-opened lids I watched the evil face bending lower and lower, until it came within a few inches of my own. I closed my eyes....

Delicate fingers touched my right eyelid as I lay like one dead. Fortunately, my medical knowledge told me what was coming—this creature sought to learn whether I was unconscious. I rolled my eyes up, as the lid was adroitly lifted and lowered again...

B-22

The man moved away. Smith murmured: "Good, Petrie! He took me on trust after that. Have you noticed the silence? Most of these men are shamming.... They are not drugged...."

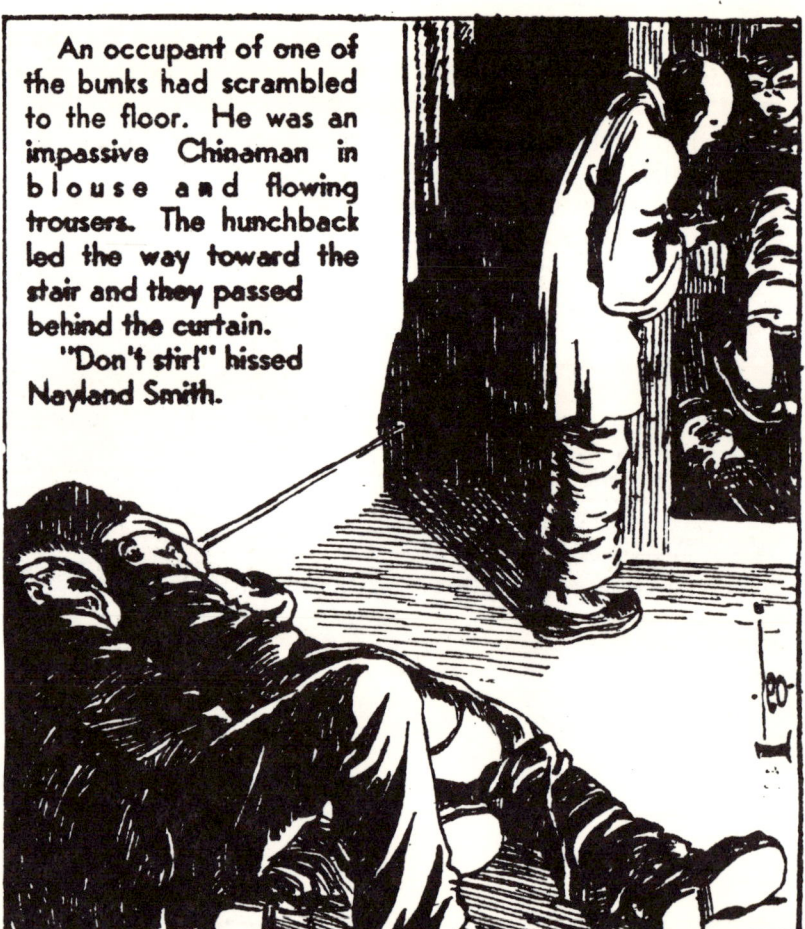

"What an awful face that man has! Petrie, it's the hunchback Detective Cadby saw going into Shen Yan's!" Suddenly he grasped my arm. "Ah, I thought so! Do you see that?"

An occupant of one of the bunks had scrambled to the floor. He was an impassive Chinaman in blouse and flowing trousers. The hunchback led the way toward the stair and they passed behind the curtain.
"Don't stir!" hissed Nayland Smith.

Soon the impassive Chinaman came downstairs and left as the little bent man went to another bunk and conducted through the curtained doorway a man who looked like a lascar.

"A dacoit!" whispered Smith excitedly. "They come here to report and take orders, Petrie. Fu Manchu is up there!"

"What shall we do?"
"Wait. We must try to rush the stairs. When that little yellow devil comes back for another man I'll give the word. You're nearer, and will have to go first, but I can deal with the hunchback...."

"Up you go, Petrie!" cried Smith, seizing the hunchback. I leaped to my feet and made for the stairs . . .

Nayland Smith was close behind me as I raced along a covered passageway in purer air, and he was at my heels when I crashed open a door at the end and almost fell into the room . . . Fu Manchu!

Fu Manchu sat at a table above which an oil-lamp swung by a brass chain. His face was dominated by the most uncanny eyes that ever reflected a human soul, for they were narrow and long, and of a brilliant green. But their unique horror lay in a certain filminess, which seemed to lift as I passed the threshold, revealing the eyes in all their weird iridescence. . . .

Fu Manchu rose as I stopped dead, for the malignant force of the man was paralyzing. Fu Manchu was surprised, yes. But no fear showed upon that evil face—only pitying contempt. . . .

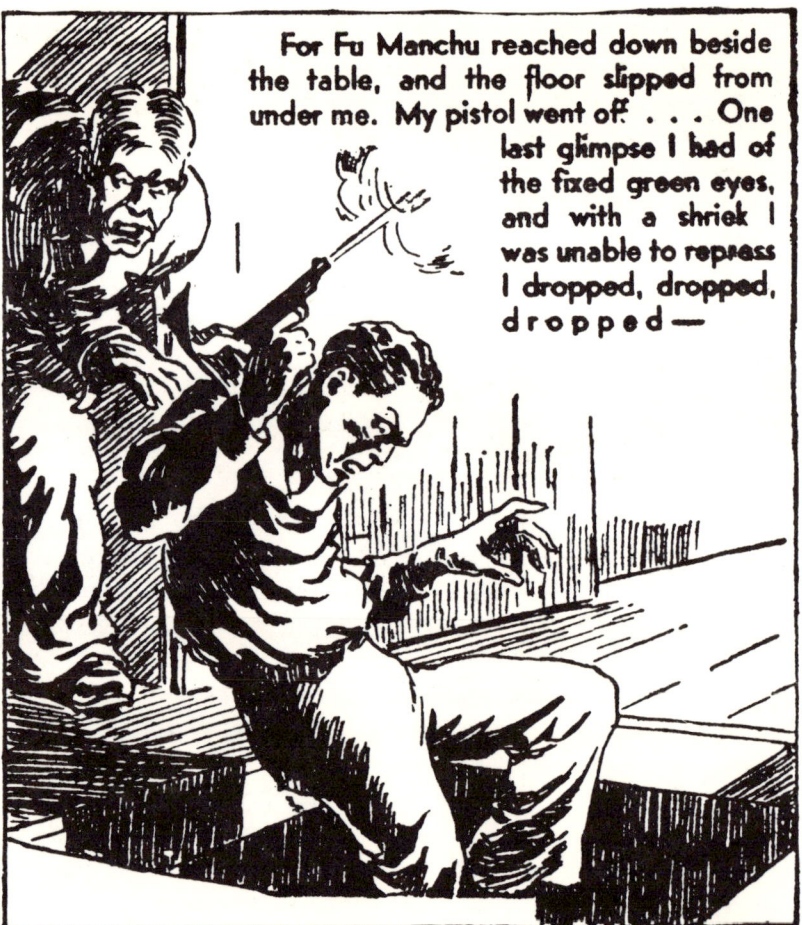

"It's Fu Manchu!" screamed Smith from behind me. "It's Fu Manchu! Cover him! Shoot him dead. . . ." The end of that sentence I never heard. . . .

For Fu Manchu reached down beside the table, and the floor slipped from under me. My pistol went off. . . . One last glimpse I had of the fixed green eyes, and with a shriek I was unable to repress I dropped, dropped, dropped—

B-25

"Smith!" I cried, "Help! Help!"
The trap which Fu Manchu had sprung as I stood before him in the upstairs room behind Shen Yan's had cast me into a pit of unknown depth, amid stifling smells and the lapping of tidal water. . . . Black terror had me by the throat. . . .

I was about to cry out again when, mustering my failing courage, I recognized that I had better use for my energies. I began to swim straight ahead — desperately determined to die hard, if die I must. . . .

A drop of liquid fire hissed into the water beside me! Another fiery drop—and another! I felt that, despite my resolution, I was going mad. . . .

I seized a rotting post. I had reached one bound of my watery prison. More fire fell. A scream of hysteria quivered in my throat.. *The floor of the room above me was in flames!*

The glow of the flames grew brighter . . . and showed me the decaying piles upholding the building, the slime-coated walls—showed me that there was no escape! By some subterranean duct my body would pass into the Thames, in the wake of Cadby, Mason, and many another victim. . . .

B-26

Swimming toward the other wall of the pit I made out rusty iron rungs affixed to one of the walls, and leading upward to another trap door than the one through which I had fallen. Hope thrilled me. . . . But the three bottom rungs of the ladder were missing!

Then the awesome light of the flames that should be my funeral pyre showed my despairing eyes something else—a projecting beam a few feet above the water—and directly beneath the iron ladder....

"Merciful Heaven!" I breathed. "Have I the strength?"

If I could grasp the beam! My garments weighed upon me like a suit of mail. A remote uproar came to my ears.... I reached for the beam....

"Petrie! Petrie!" came Smith's voice, *"Don't touch the beam!"*

"Keep afloat a few seconds more and I can get you," Nayland Smith shouted from above, "and don't touch the beam."

As my clutching fingers fell from the beam, I managed to turn, to raise my throbbing head, and saw the strangest sight of all that dreadful night....

Nayland Smith stood upon the lowest rung of the iron ladder .. supported by that hideous crookbacked Chinaman with the mask-like face who had come to us in the opium den.

"I can't reach him," Smith cried despairingly.

I saw the Chinaman snatch at his coiled pigtail and pull it off. With it came the wig to which the queue was attached. The ghastly yellow mask fell from position....

And I heard a voice I knew cry:

"Here! Here! Oh, be quick! You can-lower this to him! Be quick!"

I think my astonishment saved my life, for I clung on with what little was left of my ebbing strength, gazing upward, spellbound....

That voice! I had heard it last when its owner tricked me in Detective Cadby's rooms! Now, as Fu Manchu's slave girl bent to pass her strange life-line to Smith, a cloud of hair came falling about the slim shoulders. . . .

B-28

The girl clung to her precarious perch, leaning over to peer into the pit, while the fire roared above. I kept my gaze upturned to that beautiful, flushed face, and my eyes fixed upon hers—which were wild with fear . . . for me!

103

Smith got the pigtail into my grasp. I held to it with the strength of desperation as he slowly drew me higher and higher, until I could clasp the rung of the ladder on which he stood. . . .

Hardly had I reached the bottom rung with Smith's help and hung there sustained by his arm when the floor above burst with a mighty crash.

"As you fell through the trap your shot broke the oil lamp over Fu Manchu's head," Nayland Smith told me while we clung to the ladder. "Shen Yan's whole place is in flames. . . ."

Smith pointed into the ruddy pit.
"See that beam," he said. "Fu Manchu's devilish trap almost accounted for you, Petrie, as it did for Cadby, Mason, the dacoit and heaven knows how many more."

105

I saw in the glare of the flames, that two sword-blades, deadly keen, were riveted, edges up, along the top of the beam which only just now I had striven to grasp!
"The Severed Fingers!" I cried.

Half-fainting with the horror of what I had barely escaped, I thought only of getting out of that awful place, and turned my face upward. The trap door was open. There was no sign of the slave girl.
"Smith!" I gasped. "She's gone!"

My next recollection was of sitting up, Nayland Smith's arm about me, and Inspector Ryman holding a glass to my lips. My first confused thoughts were of the girl.

"Smith," I asked, "did you bring the pigtail with you that we found on Cadby?"

"Yes, Petrie. I hoped to meet the owner — and I did...."

B-30

"I handed it back to her after we got up the ladder and you fainted. Disguised, she managed to slip away in the excitement. I owed her your life — I had to square the account...."

Inspector Ryman had lent me a reefer, and he and Smith were helping me into a cab when another question demanded an answer of my bewildered senses.

"Fu Manchu? Did he get away...."

"There was some door at the back...." Smith replied slowly. "No one has seen him...."

"Do you think he may...."

"No," Smith rasped, "Not until I see him lying dead before me shall I believe it!"